Disney Aladdin

Ladybird

Once, in a faraway land, there lived a poor but kindhearted boy called Aladdin. He lived with his pet monkey, Abu, in the roof of an old building which overlooked the bustling marketplace of Agrabah.

Aladdin and Abu, like many others in the city, were sometimes so hungry that they had to steal food to survive – otherwise they would have starved. And they often had to run for their lives, for the Sultan's guards were always on the lookout for thieves.

The Sultan lived in a magnificent royal palace with his beautiful daughter, Princess Jasmine.

"Dearest, you must stop rejecting every suitor," pleaded the Sultan one day. "The law says you must be married to a prince by your next birthday. You have only three more days!"

"The law is *wrong*," Jasmine replied. "Oh Father, how can you force me to marry someone I do not love? I wish I hadn't been born a princess!"

"Ooooh!" cried the Sultan, shuffling angrily away.

Tears rolled down Jasmine's cheeks as she sat down and hugged her pet tiger. "I'm sorry, Rajah," she cried, "but I can't stay here any longer. I must leave."

So, early the next morning, Jasmine disguised herself, crept over the palace wall and entered Agrabah.

Jasmine wandered through the crowded, noisy market. She spotted a ragged little boy standing beside a fruit stall. "You must be hungry," she said, picking up an apple and giving it to him. "Here you go." As she turned to walk away, someone gripped her arm.

"*Thief!* You'd better be able to pay for that!" shouted the fruit seller.

"P-Pay?" Jasmine stammered. "B-But I have no money." The Princess had never before had to pay for anything in her life.

By chance, Aladdin appeared and grabbed the fruit seller's arm. "Forgive my crazy sister, kind sir," he said. "Come on, Sis, time to see the doctor."

Aladdin quickly led Jasmine to the safety of his rooftop home. "Where do you come from?" he asked.

"What does it matter?" Jasmine answered. "I ran away because my father is forcing me to get married."

"That's awful!" said Aladdin, and as he looked into Jasmine's eyes, he knew he was falling in love.

The sudden sound of heavy footsteps broke his trance. "You're under arrest!" cried one of the Sultan's guards, grabbing Aladdin's arm.

"Unhand him," said Jasmine, "by order of the Princess."

The Princess? Aladdin must have misheard.

"I would, Princess," said the chief guard, "but my orders come from Jafar."

And with that, they dragged Aladdin away to the palace dungeon.

Now, Jafar was the Sultan's most trusted adviser. But, unknown to the Sultan, he and his wicked parrot, Iago, were plotting to take over the throne. Jafar knew of a lamp that would make him the most powerful man in Agrabah.

The lamp was hidden deep in the desert in the magical Cave of Wonders. It was protected by a fierce Tiger-God. Only a person whose 'worth shone from within' could get the lamp – Aladdin!

So, disguised as an old, broken-toothed prisoner, Jafar freed Aladdin from the dungeon and led him to the massive jaws of the cave. "Bring me the lamp," he ordered, "and you shall have your reward."

"Proceed!" roared the Tiger-God. "Touch *nothing* but the lamp!"

The words rang in Aladdin's ears as he and Abu entered the cave. They followed steep steps down, down, until they found a huge chamber filled with mountains of golden treasure and jewels.

Suddenly, Aladdin noticed a richly embroidered carpet peeking at them from behind a pile of gold coins. "A magic carpet," laughed Aladdin. "Maybe it can show us where the lamp is."

The carpet whirled round and began pointing excitedly towards a second chamber. There, across a lake of brilliant blue, at the top of a tall tower, was the lamp.

"Don't touch *anything,* Abu," warned Aladdin as he raced up the tower steps. But Abu wasn't listening. He had spotted a giant ruby in the hands of a golden statue. He just couldn't resist it!

As Abu's tiny paws gripped the jewel, the voice of the Tiger-God echoed round the mighty chamber. "You have touched the forbidden treasure. Now you will never again see the light of day." At once, the ground started to shake and the shimmering lake of blue turned into a pool of boiling, red lava.

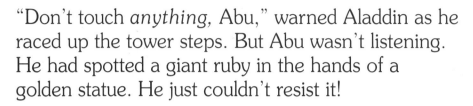

The tower, where Aladdin was standing, began to crumble. He snatched the lamp, ran down the swaying stairs and jumped on board the carpet. As the cave collapsed around them, Aladdin reached over and plucked Abu from danger.

Eventually the earthquake stopped and the lava disappeared. Aladdin looked at Abu and the carpet. He knew they were all trapped.

"I wonder what's so special about this dusty, old thing anyway," said Aladdin, as he tried to rub the side of the lamp clean. He rubbed harder and harder – then stopped. The lamp was glowing!

Poooof! Smoke poured from its spout, whirling crazily into a blue cloud. The cloud slowly formed into an enormous shape with arms, a chest and a face which suddenly spoke: "Hi! I'm your Genie, direct from the lamp. Right here to grant you three wishes."

Aladdin decided to tease the Genie a little. "An all-powerful Genie?" he said. "I bet you can't even get us out of this cave."

"I'll soon see about that!" said the Genie. And, quick as a wink, they were flying high above the desert on the magic carpet.

"How's that?" asked the Genie, guiding the carpet down to land by an oasis near Agrabah. "Am I a Genie, or am I a Genie?"

"You're a Genie, all right," laughed Aladdin. "Now, about my three wishes?"

"Okay," said the Genie. "But no more freebies, and no fair wishing for three more wishes!"

Aladdin thought of Princess Jasmine. "Genie, I wish…" said Aladdin aloud, "I wish to be a prince!" With a sweeping wave of the Genie's arm, Aladdin was suddenly dressed, from turban to toe, in the finest silks and jewels of a royal prince.

The Genie then led a magnificent procession down
the main street of Agrabah towards the Sultan's palace.
"Prince Ali Ababwa!" announced a guard, as the palace
gates were thrown open. Into the throne
room flew Aladdin on his magic carpet.

"Your Majesty, I have come to seek the
hand of Princess Jasmine," he said.

That evening, Prince Ali took Jasmine
for a moonlit ride on the magic carpet.
He reminded Jasmine of the boy
in the marketplace. But Jafar
had said that boy had been
beheaded. Whoever Prince
Ali was, Jasmine had
fallen in love with him.

As they said good night,
Jasmine knew this was the
prince she wanted to marry.

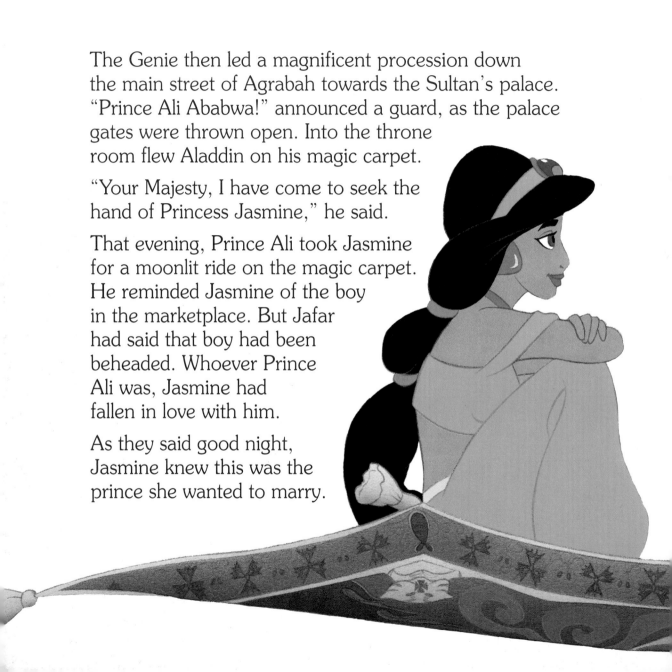

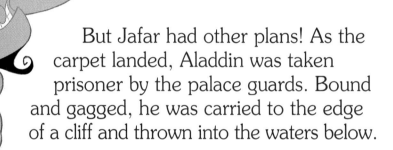

But Jafar had other plans! As the carpet landed, Aladdin was taken prisoner by the palace guards. Bound and gagged, he was carried to the edge of a cliff and thrown into the waters below.

As Aladdin dropped like a stone to the bottom of the sea, the lamp fell from his turban. He struggled against the chains, but it was no good – he couldn't quite reach.

Then, as if by magic, the lamp gently rolled towards Aladdin and touched his hand. The Genie appeared. "I guess your second wish is that I get you out of this mess!" he said. Barely conscious, Aladdin nodded.

Back at the palace, Jasmine wanted to tell her father how happy she was. But before she could say a word, the Sultan spoke. "Jasmine," he droned, "you will... marry... Jafar." The snake's head on Jafar's staff glowed, working its hypnotic spell.

"Never! I have chosen Prince Ali," cried Jasmine. "Father, what's wrong with you?"

"I know!" said a voice from the window. No one had noticed Aladdin enter the room. "Your Highness," he continued, "Jafar's been controlling you with this." Aladdin snatched the staff and smashed it on the floor.

Jafar ran from the room, but not before he had seen the lamp in Aladdin's turban. At dawn the next morning, Iago flew into Aladdin's room and stole the lamp.

Hiding in his laboratory, Jafar eagerly took the lamp from the parrot.

"I am your master now!" bellowed Jafar, as he rubbed the lamp and watched the Genie appear. "My first wish is to be Sultan. My second wish is to be the most powerful sorcerer in the world."

"I don't like it, but you've got it," said the Genie.

At once, Jafar's wishes were granted. With an evil laugh, he turned to the Princess. "Look at your precious Prince Ali now – or should we say, Aladdin?" he sneered. Suddenly, Aladdin was dressed again in his rags.

Using more of his magical powers, Jafar transformed the Sultan into a tiny puppet hanging from the ceiling. Rajah was turned into a kitten.

"Bring me more wine, slave!" Jafar ordered Jasmine. Helpless under the sorcerer's power, the Princess obeyed.

Then lightning shot from Jafar's fingertips, and sharp swords fell from the ceiling towards Aladdin.

"I'm not finished yet, you cowardly snake," cried Aladdin, bravely dodging the swords. He picked one up and charged at the wicked sorcerer.

"A snake, am I?" replied Jafar, avoiding the blow. "Perhaps you'd like to see how snakelike I can be!" Instantly, Jafar turned himself into a massive cobra with huge, deadly fangs.

Aladdin thought quickly. "You're not powerful," he shouted. "The Genie's given you everything! He has more power than you'll ever have."

"You're right!" hissed Jafar. "Slave, I have chosen my final wish. Make me an all-powerful genie."

Swirling smoke filled the room. The cobra vanished and Jafar reappeared in the shape of a gigantic genie. "Now I have absolute power!" he cried.

Gold shackles suddenly clamped round his wrists. His legs became a trail of vapour, and a lamp appeared beneath him. "What's happening?" Jafar demanded.

"You wanted to be a genie," said Aladdin. "Well, you've got your wish – and everything that goes with it."

Jafar and Iago were sucked into the lamp for ever. Slowly, everything in the palace returned to normal.

"I'm sorry I lied to you about being a prince," Aladdin said to Jasmine. "I guess this is goodbye?"

"But I love you!" cried the Princess. "If only it wasn't for that stupid law."

"You still have your final wish," the Genie reminded Aladdin. "Just say the word and you're a prince again."

But Aladdin knew how much the Genie longed to be free. "I wish for your freedom," said Aladdin. In a flash, the Genie's gold cuffs vanished! "I'm going to miss you, Al," the Genie cried, as he flew off to start a new life. "You'll always be a prince to me."

"That's right," agreed the Sultan. "You've certainly proved your worth. What we need is a new law. From today, the Princess may marry whomever she wishes."

And, of course, as Jasmine wished to marry Aladdin, that's exactly what she did!

Ladybird books are widely available, but in case of difficulty may be ordered by post or telephone from:
Ladybird Books – Cash Sales Department Littlegate Road Paignton Devon TQ3 3BE Telephone 0803 554761

A catalogue record for this book is available from the British Library

Published by Ladybird Books Ltd Loughborough Leicestershire UK
LADYBIRD and the device of a Ladybird are trademarks of Ladybird Books Ltd